W. H. Smith

Grammar Made Easy

W. H. Smith

Grammar Made Easy

ISBN/EAN: 9783337393069

Printed in Europe, USA, Canada, Australia, Japan

Cover: Foto ©Andreas Hilbeck / pixelio.de

More available books at **www.hansebooks.com**

Grammar Made Easy,

FOR THOSE

Who have never Learned anything relating to
Grammar, and for those who in early years
have Learnt its Rules, but have neglected
or forgotten to practice them.

IT BEING A

COMPLETE MANUAL OF INSTRUCTION

FOR

CORRECT SPEAKING, WRITING AND SPELLING FOR ADULTS.

NEW YORK:
HURST & CO., PUBLISHERS,
75 AND 77 NASSAU STREET.

CONTENTS.

Entered according to Act of Congress, in the year 1873, by Hurst & Co., in the office of the Librarian of Congress, at Washington, D. C.

GRAMMAR MADE EASY.

INTRODUCTION.

GRAMMAR is the science which treats of the principles and rules of spoken and written language; and teaches the proper use of letters, syllables, words, and sentences.

The object of English grammar is to teach those who use the English language to express their thoughts correctly, either in speaking or writing.

Dr. Blair, in his "Lectures on Rhetoric," says :—"The structure of language is extremely artificial; and there are few sciences in which a deeper or more refined logic is employed than in grammar. It is apt to be slighted by superficial thinkers, as belonging to those rudiments of knowledge which were inculcated upon us in our earliest youth. But what was then inculcated before we could comprehend its principles would abundantly repay our study in maturer years."

But few persons can afford time for the study of grammar, and perhaps fewer still have the inclination. The English language is, without doubt, the most neglected, and carelessly spoken and written, language in Europe. Tenfold the time and attention that is given to it is devoted by the educated classes to the study of Greek and Latin; and it may be truly affirmed that there are more men in England who can write Greek and Latin *correctly* than who can write English. An Oxford examiner states, in the "Public Schools' Report," that in one of the examinations *In Literis Humanioribus*, "nearly half the passmen were imperfect spellers," and that "five-sixths of the pupil-teachers in schools receiving aid from Government are better readers than five-sixths of the men who come to the University." Another examiner says :—"I have had sometimes to remind myself and my brother examiners that we were not at liberty to pluck for bad spelling, bad English, or worse writing." Many of these men would enter the Senate, the Bar, and the Church, and help to spread a careless and incorrect style.

It is highly useful, from time to time, to refresh the memory with "rules" which tend to make us careful, even if they do not make us perfect. To give the chief rules in a plain and brief form, so that "all who run may read," is the object of this little work. Dr. Campbell, in his "Philosophy of Rhetoric," justly says:—"The rules of our language should breathe the same spirit as the laws of our country. They should be bars against licentiousness, without being checks to liberty."

DIVISIONS OF GRAMMAR.

English Grammar is divided usually into four parts, namely Orthography, Etymology, Syntax, and Prosody.

Orthography treats of letters, and of the mode of combining them into syllables and words. But Orthography is the province of the lexicographer, rather than the grammarian, and a breach of it is not even called bad grammar. However, we shall give concise rules for spelling plurals, etc., correctly, and directions for acquiring correct Orthography as of the highest importance to every one.

Etymology treats of the various classes of words, and of the changes which they undergo. But only one branch of it, namely, the inflexions of words, or changes in their determinations, is usually included in Grammar; Derivation being a separate study.

Syntax treats of the connection of words and their arrangement into sentences.

Prosody treats of the quantity or length of syllables, of accent, and of the laws of versification. Some grammarians consider that it should include Punctuation, or the management of stops, Pronunciation and Rhetoric. But we think that Punctuation should form a fifth division, while Pronunciation properly belongs to Elocution, and Rhetoric to Composition.

PARTS OF SPEECH.

There are in English nine classes of words, or, as they are commonly called, Parts of Speech, namely :—

1. The Article; prefixed to substantives or nouns, to point them out, and to show how far their signification extends.

2. The Substantive, or Noun; being the name of any person, place, or thing conceived to exist, or of which we have any notion.

3. The Pronoun (from *pro*, for); used instead of a noun, to avoid repetition. ·

4. The Adjective; *added* to the noun, to express its quality or property.

5. The Verb, or Word (from *Verbum*, a word), so called by way of eminence; signifying to be, to do, or to suffer.

6. The Adverb; *added* to verbs, and also to adjectives, and other adverbs, to express some circumstance of quality or action belonging to them.

7. The Preposition (from *pre*, before); put before nouns and pronouns chiefly, to connect them with other words, and to show their relation to those words.

8. The Conjunction; connecting words and sentences.

9. The Interjection; thrown in to express the emotion of the speaker, though unnecessary with respect to the construction of the sentence.

EXAMPLE.

1	2	7	2	5	1	2		4	7	2	8	5

The power of speech is a faculty peculiar to man, and was

5	7	3	7	3	4	2	7	1	4	8

bestowed on him by his beneficent Creator for the greatest and

6	4	2	8	9	6	6	5	3	5	3	7

most excellent uses; but alas! how often do we pervert it to

1	4	7	2

the worst of purposes.

In the foregoing sentence, the words *the, a*, are Articles; *power speech, faculty, man, Creator, uses, purposes*, are Substantives; *him, his, we, it*, are Pronouns; *peculiar, beneficent, greatest, excellent, worst*, are Adjectives; *is, was, bestowed, do, pervert*, are Verbs; *most, how, often*, are Adverbs; *of, to, on, by, for*, are Prepositions; *and, but*, are Conjunctions; and *alas !* is an Interjection.

THE ARTICLE.

In English there are two articles, *a* or *an*, and *the*. *A* is used in a vague sense to point out one single thing of the kind, in other respects indeterminate; *the* determines what particular thing is meant.

A substantive, without any article to limit it, is taken in its widest sense : thus *man* means all mankind ; as,

" The proper study of mankind is man."—POPE.

Where *mankind* and *man* may change places, without making any alteration in the sense. A *man* means some one or other of that kind, indefinitely ; *the man* means, definitely, that particular man, who is spoken of : the former therefore is called the Indefinite, the latter the Definite Article.

For example : " *Man* was made for society, and ought to extend his good will to all *men :* but *a man* will naturally entertain a more particular kindness for *the men* with whom he has the most frequent intercourse ; and enter into a still closer union with *the man* whose temper and disposition suit best with his own."

It is of the nature of both the articles to determine or limit the thing spoken of : *a* determines it to be one single thing of the kind, leaving it still uncertain which ; *the* determines which it is, or, of many, which they are. The first, therefore, can only be joined to substantives in the singular number; the last may also be joined to plurals.

There is a remarkable exception to this rule in the use of the adjectives *few* and *many* (the latter chiefly with the word *great* before it), which though joined with plural substantives, yet admit of the singular article *a ;* as, A *few men*, a *great many men*. The reason of it is manifest from the effect which the article has in these phrases; it means a small or great number collectively taken, and therefore gives the idea of a whole that is of unity. Thus likewise, *a hundred, a thousand*, is one whole number, an aggregate of many collectively taken, which like *a dozen*, or *a score*, we are accustomed equally to consider on certain occasions as a simple unity ; and therefore still retains the article *a*, though joined as an adjective to a plural substantive ; as, *A hundred years*.

A is frequently used to denote a rate or proportion ; as, Five hundred *a* year, three dollars *a* bottle, and is sometimes prefixed to the present participle of active verbs ; as, Gone *a*-hunting, come *a*-begging.

The definite article *the* is sometimes applied to adverbs in the comparative and superlative degree; and its effect is to mark the degree the more strongly, and to define it the more precisely; as, " *The more* I examine it, *the better* I like it." "I like this *the least* of any."

When the indefinite article is to be placed before a noun, *a* or *an* is employed according as the one or the other can be more readily formed by the organs of speech, and is more pleasing to the ear when pronounced along with the word which follows. Therefore, *a* is used before words beginning with a consonant, the sounds of *w* and *y*, and the long sound of *u;* as, *A* book, *a* word *a* youth, many *a* one (wun), *a* European, *a* unit, *a* eulogy, *a* ewe. The pronunciation of *y* or *w* at the beginning of a word, requires such an effort in the conformation of the parts of the mouth, as does not easily admit of the article *an* before them. In other cases the article *an* in a manner coalesces with the vowel which it precedes: in this, the effort of pronunciation separates the article, and prevents the disagreeable consequences of a sensible hiatus.

An is used before words beginning with vowel, as, *An* army; silent *h*, as *An* hour; and before *h* sounded when the accent is on the second syllable, to avoid the hiatus, as, *An* hallu'cination, *an* Hercu'lean frame, *an* hered'itary estate, *an* hero'ic or hero'ical action, *an* hia'tus, *an* histor'ic or histor'ical account, *an* hydrau'lic ram, etc.

THE SILENT *H.*

Although the pronunciation of the aspirate or letter *h*, properly belongs to that branch of Elocution called Orthoepy, it is here advisable to give a list of the words in which the *h* is silent.

The *h* in each of the following words and their other derivatives was formerly silent: heir, heiress, heirloom; herb, herbage; honest, honesty, honestly; honor, honorable, honorably, honorary; hospital; hostler; hour, hourly; humor, humorist, humorously; humble, humility; and to aspirate any of them was considered as gross a fault as to prefix an aspirate to a vowel. But the fashion of pronunciation has altered, and some of these words are now aspirated. Nevertheless, great difference of opinion exists among the best authorities. Smart aspirates "herb," and all its derivatives, but Dr. Noah Webster, while aspirating all the derivatives, most inconsistently makes the *h* silent in "herb." Smart makes the *h* silent in "hostler," while Dr. Webster aspirates the word, very properly, we think, for it is a corruption of "hosteller," an inn-keeper, or host of an inn. "Humble," is now aspirated by the most highly educated and refined.

We know of no good reason why any of the above few words should be deprived of the aspirate, and pronounced differently to their fellows, but as all-potent custom denies the aspirate to them, we must obey. But however desirable it would be to remove all these exceptions, so powerful is habit in pronunciation, that to aspirate some of these words at present, would be highly unpleasant to a polished ear. Nevertheless, when custom changes, as in the above instances, we think it well to follow, in this case, a good example, for by so doing, we may, in course of time, remove the few exceptions which trouble many persons without improving the language.

We would therefore limit the silent *h* to the following words, upon which nearly all authorities are agreed : heir, heiress, heirloom ; honest, honesty, honestly ; honor, honorable, honorably, honorary ; hour, hourly ; humor humorous, humorously, and their other derivatives.

"Humble-pie" is an incorrect spelling of "umble-pie," a pie made of "umbles," a plural noun, meaning a deer's entrails, probably derived from the Latin *umbilicus*, the "navel." "Umbilic," was once used, substantively for the "navel." Thus, to "eat umble-pie," is to eat of the poorest dish. The *h* is a wrong spelling, and should be omitted.

"Humble-bee," a bee of a large kind, with no sting, corruptly called "bumble-bee" in some parts of the country, is not related to the word "humble," signifying "humility," but is derived from the verb "to hum," and consequently has always had the *h* aspirated. "Humming-bird" is derived from the same verb.

NOUNS

Are inflected, or changed in their form, by Number, Gender, and Case, to express their various relations to the things which they represent, and to other words in the same sentence.

The English language, in comparison with the Greek, Latin, German, and French, and many other languages, has very few inflections. Its general deficiency in this respect is compensated by the more frequent use of pronouns, prepositions, etc.

Inflection is not necessarily confined to the end of the word, but is often made in the word: as, Man, men; mouse, mice; spring, sprang.

FORMATION OF THE PLURAL.

Number is that inflection by which we indicate, whether the word represents one, or more than one.

There are two Numbers, the Singular, which expresses one of a kind, and the Plural, which expresses more than one.

Nouns generally form the plural by adding the letter *s* to the singular, when the letter *s* readily combines in sound with the last letter or syllable; as, Book, books; pen, pens.

But when the letter *s* does not readily combine in sound with the last letter or syllable of the singular, the plural is formed by adding *es*. Thus, nouns ending in *ch* soft, *sh*, *ss*, *s*, *x*, or *o* after a consonant, take *es* instead of *s* only; as, Church, churches; brush, brushes; kiss, kisses; omnibus, omnibuses; fox, foxes; hero, heroes.

The following words ending in *o* after a consonant are exceptions to the rule, and form their plural by adding *s* only:—Canto, grotto, junto, portico, octavo, quarto, solo, tyro.

Nouns ending in *ch* hard, and in *o* preceded by a vowel, form the plural by adding *s* only; as, Monarch, monarchs; folio, folios.

Nouns ending in *f* or *fe* change *f* or *fe* into *ves*; as, Calf, calves; knife, knives; leaf, leaves.

Except the following terminations, which are regular, and take *s* only:—*oof*, as Roof, roofs; *ief*, as Chief, chiefs; *ff*, as Muff, muffs; *rf*, as Wharf, wharfs; and two ending in *fe*, namely, strife, strifes; fife, fifes. Thief makes thieves.

Nouns ending in *y* preceded by a consonant, change *y* into *ies*; as, Duty, duties; glory, glories.

In like manner the word alkali has alkalies in the plural. But nouns ending in *y* preceded by a vowel, and proper names used as common nouns, follow the general rule, and add only *s*; as, Day, days; valley, valleys; Henry, Henrys.

Few words are so often erroneously spelled as those ending in *y* or *ey*, when they change that form to become plural.

Some authors and printers still write and print a few words ending in *ey* in the singular with *ies* when plural; as, Attorney, attornies ; chimney, chimnies ; journey, journies ; money, monies ; volley, vollies.

Many nouns do not follow the preceding rules, and are therefore called irregular; as, Man, men ; child, children ; foot, feet, etc.

Such words as aide-de-camp, court-martial, son-in-law, etc., from the plural by changing the first word only ; as, Aides-de-camp, courts-martial, sons-in-law, etc.

The compounds of man, namely, alderman, footman, woman, etc., form the plural, like the simple word, by changing a in the singular into e in the plural ; as, Aldermen, footmen, women, etc.

Such words as Mussulman, Turcoman, are not compounds of man, but distinct words, and form the plural by adding s.

Some nouns vary the plural to express a difference of meaning ; as, Brother, brothers (sons of the same parent), brethren (members of the same faith or profession) ; die, dies (stamps for coining), dice (small cubes used in games) ; genius, geniuses (persons of great, original, and creative intellect), genii (spirits) ; index, indexes (tables of contents) ; indices (signs in Algebra) ; pea, peas (single seeds) ; pease (seeds in a mass) ; penny, pennies (coins), pence (value of coins in computation).

Nouns which have been adopted from foreign languages without change, sometimes retain their original plurals ; as, Animalcuium, animalcula ; appendix, appendices ; bandit, banditti ; basis, bases ; beau, beaux ; cherub, cherubim ; criterion, criteria ; crisis crises ; datum, data ; desideratum, desiderata ; effluvium, effluvia ; ellipsis, ellipses ; erratum, errata ; focus, foci ; genus, genera ; hypothesis, hypotheses ; medium, media ; memorandum, memoranda ; metamorphosis, metamorphoses ; monsieur, messieurs ; phenomenon, phenomena ; radius, radii ; seraph, seraphim ; stimulus, stimuli ; stratum, strata ; vertex, vertices ; virtuoso, virtusoi ; vortex, vortices.   Cherubs and seraphs are also correct.

Many nouns have no plural : these are chiefly proper names, names of virtues and vices, arts and sciences, metals, grain, and things that can be weighed and measured ; as, America, New York ; wisdom, goodness ; poetry, music, arithmetic ; gold, silver ; wheat, barley ; meat, butter ; beer, milk, etc.

However, when the different kinds are meant, ale, tea, wine, etc., are, in commercial language, often used in the plural ; as, Fine ales, old wines, new teas, etc. So also when particular acts are signified ; as, Kindnesses.

Some nouns have no singular number ; as, Bellows, drawers, mathematics, thanks, scissors, etc.

Among this class of words are to be reckoned letters, signifying literature and manners in the sense of behavior. Amends, means, odds, are either singular or plural. News is generally used as singular ; likewise alms and gallows.

Some nouns have the singular and plural the same; as, Brace, dozen, score, swine, salmon, etc. Others take *a* to make the singular ; as, *a* deer. It is incorrect to say three pairs of boots, five dozens of wine. But the plural form is used when there is no word to limit the number ; as, Dozens of gloves, scores of presents, hundreds of people.

The proper plurals of the words spoonful, mouthful, and suchlike, are spoonfuls, mouthfuls, and not spoonsful, mouthsful. Between these and the preceding there is an essential difference, for "Two large spoonfuls of this mixture to be taken," implies that twice the quantity a spoon will hold is to be taken ; but " Two large spoonsful of this mixture to be taken," may signify that the spoons also are to be swallowed. " Spoonsful " must be many spoons full ; but " spoonfuls " means many contents of one spoon. " Spoonful " is a distinct word, and forms its plural regularly like ordinary words. In Johnson's dictionary the word "spoonful" is given as a substantive, and all substantives which form their plurals regularly, do so by adding an *s* at the end and not in the middle of the word. In like manner five wine-glassesful would mean five different glasses full ; but five wine-glassfuls means five times the contents of one glass.

The same rule will apply to other words of a similar class ; as, Handful, handfuls ; pailful, pailfuls ; puncheonful, puncheonfuls ; hundredweight, hundredweights.

GENDERS OF NOUNS.

Properly speaking, there are only two genders, the masculine and the feminine, corresponding to the two sexes ; but as many nouns belong to neither sex, these are classed together, and denominated neuter, that is, of neither gender.

When a noun may be applied either to a male or a female, it is said to be of the common gender ; as, Parent, child, friend.

There are three ways of distinguishing the masculine from the feminine :

1. By a different ending ; as, Duke, duchess.
2. By a different word ; as, Husband, wife.
3. By prefixing a noun, an adjective, or a pronoun ; as, Man-servant, maid-servant ; male-child, female-child ; he-goat, she-goat.

Some neuter nouns may be used as masculine or feminine, by a figure of speech, called personification. Thus we say of the sun, "*he* is rising ; " of the moon, "*she* is setting ; " and of a ship, "*she* sails well."

The sun, time, death, summer, winter, autumn, love, and similar words, when personified, are masculine.

The moon, religion, virtue (and all particular virtues ; as, charity), the earth, spring, a ship, a state, a city, a country (and all particular countries), the soul, the mind, and similar words, when personified, are feminine.

In speaking of animals in a general manner, we attribute the masculine sex to some, and the feminine to others, although they really possess both. Thus the ass, the eagle, the dog, the fox, the horse, the lion, etc., are spoken of as masculine ; while the cat, the camel, the hare, the ostrich, are generally considered as feminine.

Most of the smaller creatures, with reptiles and fishes, are usually spoken of as neuter. But there are some exceptions ; and most of those animals that have been made the subjects of popular fables, have had a particular gender ascribed to them.

CASES OF NOUNS.

There are three cases of nouns in English, the Nominative, the Possessive, and the Objective ; which three cases are expressive of the three states of relation to other words, in one or other of which the name of every person, place, or thing must be placed.

A noun is in the nominative case when it is the subject of an affirmation or a question.

A noun is in the possessive case when it expresses ownership or *possession.*

A noun is in the objective case when it is the end or *object* of an action, or of some relation expressed by a preposition.

Thus, in the example, "John took Robert's knife, and put it

into the pocket of William's coat," two affirmations are made by the verbs *took* and *put*. The subject of these affirmations, or the person who *took* and *put*, was John, whose name is, therefore, in the nominative case. The object or end of John's action in taking, was the *knife;* the object pointed out by the preposition *into* was the *pocket;* and the object pointed out by the preposition *of*, was *coat;* the words *knife, pocket*, and *coat*, are therefore in the objective case. The owner of the knife was *Robert*, and the owner of the coat was *William;* hence the words *Robert's* and *William's* are in the possessive case.

The nominative and the objective cases of nouns are always alike in form, in English.

The possessive singular and the possessive plural are the most important to be noticed, as showing more particularly where the apostrophe (') should be placed; that is, whether *before* or *after* the *s*. Mistakes in this respect are often made by educated people.

The possessive singular is formed by *adding* an apostrophe and *s* to the nominative; as, Queen, queen's; the scholar's books.

If the apostrophe were placed *after* the *s* in "The scholar's books," thus: "The scholars' books," it would imply several scholars.

When the nominative singular ends in *s*, *ss*, *cc*, or any other letter or syllable which will not combine in sound with *s*, the possessive is formed by adding an apostrophe only; as, Moses' rod, for righteousness' sake, for conscience' sake.

The possessive plural is formed by *adding* an apostrophe to the nominative plural when the latter ends in *s;* as, Kings, kings', on eagles' wings. It may be observed that, "on eagles' wings" implies any number of eagles, but if the apostrophe were placed *before* the *s*, it would then mean one eagleonly.

But when the nominative plural does not end in *s*, the possessive is formed by adding *s after* an apostrophe; as, Men, men's; the children's books.

When two or more nouns in the possessive case are closely joined, the apostrophe and *s*, or *s* and apostrophe, is annexed only to the last, and understood as to the rest; as, Shakespeare and Milton's works. But if several words intervene, the *'s* or *s'* is added to each; as, He took his father's, as well as his mother's advice.

It is a common but gross error to write pronouns in the possessive case with an apostrophe before the *s ;* as, *her's* for *hers ; their's* for *theirs ; our's* for *ours ; your's* for *yours.* The *s* alone, without the apostrophe, is sufficient, that letter in these words denoting the possessive case. *Her, their*, etc., describe possession, and the *s* is merely annexed to indicate the omission of the implied name that would have appeared if the *s* had been omitted. It would be as reasonable to write *plurals* or *others* with an apostrophe, thus—*plural's, other's*—as to write *her's* and *their's* for *hers* and *theirs.* -

Mr. Davidson says: "A similar, yet more irrational practice, is followed up by the prevalent use of *your's* and *yours'*, respectively. It is a wild fancy, indeed, to imagine that *yours*, which is on all hands allowed to be plural, can be curtailed or lengthened at pleasure, to mean either one or two, by the mere position of the apostrophe. This error is more frequently found at the conclusion of letters after this manner;—' I am, sir, your's, etc.; ' or, ' I am, gentlemen, yours', etc.' Probably it is the practice of placing the apostrophe before and after what has been called the possessive case of names, for the singular and plural, that has led to this violation, but this reduces the thing to a still more pitiable condition, for the spelling of *your* itself indicates *possession* equally with the *'s*, and therefore *your's* or *yours'* involves the absurdity of a double possessive."

COMPARISON OF ADJECTIVES.

Adjectives have three forms :—the Positive, which does not express comparison ; as, A *rich* man.

The Comparative, which expresses comparison between two, or between one and a number taken collectively ; as, John is *richer* than James : he is *richer* than all the merchants in New York.

The Superlative, which expresses comparison between one and a number of individuals, or things taken separately ; as, John is the *richest* man in New York. It is the *finest* house in the street.

The comparative is formed by adding *er* to the positive ; as, Great, great*er ;* small, small*er*.

When the positive ends in *e*, the letter *r* only is added ; as, Large, larg*er*.

The superlative is formed by adding *est* to the positive ; as, Great, great*est ;* small, small*est*.

When the positive ends in *e* the letters *st* only are added ; as, large, large*st.*

When the positive ends in *y* preceded by a consonant, the *y* is changed into *i* before *er* and *est ;* as, Happy, happi*er,* happi*est.*

When the positive ends in a single consonant, preceded by a single vowel, the consonant is doubled before *er* and *est ;* as, Hot, hot*ter,* hott*est.*

Adjectives of one syllable, and dissyllables ending in *y* and *e* usually form the comparative and superlative according to the preceding rules, but all other adjectives of two syllables, and adjectives of more than two syllables, usually form the comparative and superlative by prefixing *more* and *most ;* as, Useful, *more* useful, *most* useful. This is a modern practice. In Milton, for instance, we find famousest, virtuousest, etc. A few adjectives form the superlative by adding *most* to the positive or comparative ; as, Fore, fore*most ;* upper, upper*most.*

Many grammarians object to the addition of the comparative and superlative terms when the adjective already expresses the highest degree ; as, Chief, empty, false, honest, complete, extreme, full, perfect, supreme, true, universal, etc. Yet some of these forms are found in most languages, and in our own old authors. Not only Bacon, Spenser, and Shakespeare, but later writers, Dryden and Addison, use *extremest ;* and there is equal authority for *chiefest* and *more perfect.* But such forms, although authorized by great and classic writers, are best avoided, as being logically incorrect. They are not generally employed by our best modern authors.

The adverb *very* is often prefixed to the positive to increase its signification by expressing a degree of quality somewhat less than the greatest or superlative degree ; as, Wise, *very* wise.

A form used to express a very high degree of any quality, without directly comparing the object with any other, by prefixing an adverb or adjective in the superlative degree, as, An *extremely* fine day, a *most* beautiful garden, is called the superlative of eminence, or superlative absolute.

The syllable *ish* is sometimes added to the positive to lessen its signification ; as, Black, black*ish.* When the positive ends in *e,* the *e* is omitted before *ish ;* as, White, whit*ish.* A degree somewhat less than the positive may also be expressed without direct comparison, by prefixing an adverb ; as, *Rather* salt, *somewhat* sour.

And the lower and lowest degrees may be expressed by prefixing the adverbs *less* and *least;* as, *Less* useful, *least* useful. This is called the comparison of diminution.

Elder and *eldest* are applied to persons; and according to the best authorities only in comparing members of the same family; as, An *elder* brother; the *eldest* sister; he is the *eldest* of the family.

Older and *oldest* are applied to strangers and to things; as, John is *older* than Thomas; it is the *oldest* house in the town.

The following adjectives are irregular in the formation of the comparative and superlative :—

POSITIVE.	COMPARATIVE.	SUPERLATIVE.
Bad, Evil, Ill,	worse,	worst.
Far,	farther, further,	farthest, furthest.
Fore,	former,	foremost, first.
Good,	better,	best.
Hind,	hinder,	hindmost, hindermost.
In,	inner,	inmost, innermost.
Late,	later, latter,	latest, last.
Little,	less,	least.
Low,	lower,	lowest, lowermost.
Many, Much,	more,	most.
Near,	nearer,	nearest, next.
——	nether,	nethermost.
Old,	elder, older,	eldest, oldest.
Out,	outer,	outermost, utmost.
——	under,	undermost.
Up,	upper,	uppermost, upmost.

Farther is applied to distance, *further* to quantity; as, He walked *farther* than you. *Further* funds are wanted.

PERSONAL PRONOUNS

Are so called because they are used instead of the names of persons, places, and things, to avoid the repetition of the noun for which they are put.

The personal pronouns are *I, thou, he, she,* and *it,* with their inflections, my, me ; thy, thee ; his, him ; her ; its ; our, us ; your, you ; their, them.

I, which is used when a person speaks of himself, is called the pronoun of the *first* person.

Thou or *you,* used in speaking to another, is called the pronoun of the *second* person.

He, she, and *it,* used in speaking of a person or thing, are called the pronouns of the *third* person.

Thou is seldom used except in addressing the Deity.

You is now used both as the singular and plural of the second person. *Ye* is the old form of the nominative plural, and is chiefly used in the Bible and dramatic works.

We is often used instead of *I* by sovereigns, authors, and public speakers. With sovereigns it is a sign of royalty. In order to avoid the appearance of egotism, *I* ought to be employed as little as possible in literary composition.

It may be used not only in place of the name of an object, but instead of a clause of a sentence ; as, " *It* is the scholar's duty to learn his lessons well," instead of " *To learn his lessons well* is the scholar's duty." In such expressions as, *It* rains, *it* freezes, it does not stand for either a noun or a clause of a sentence, but is used to point out the effect of some cause not specified.

My, thy, her, our, your, and *their* are used when the name of the person or thing possessed is mentioned immediately after them ; as, *My* book, *your* pen, *her* dress. *Mine, thine, hers, ours, yours,* and *theirs* are used when the name of the person or thing possessed is mentioned in a previous part of the sentence, or is only understood ; as, The book is *mine ;* the pen is *yours.* Whose is that dress ? *Hers.*

Mine and *thine* were formerly used for *my* and *thy* before a vowel or *h* mute ; as, *Mine* eyes, *mine* own ; *thine* ears ; *thine* heir.

The word *own* is sometimes added to the possessives *my, mine, thine, his, her, its, our, your,* and *their,* to render them more empathic; as, *My own* book ; it is *your own* fault.

Self, in the plural *selves,* is also added to the possessive case of pronouns of the first and second persons, and to the objective of pronouns of the third person ; as, *Myself, ourselves ; himself, themselves.* These are called Reciprocal Pronouns, because, when used after verbs, they denote that the agent and the object of the action are the same ; as, *They* injure *themselves.*

RELATIVE PRONOUNS

Are so called because they relate to some word or clause going before, which is called *Antecedent.* They are *who, which, that,* and *what.*

Who is applied to persons only ; as, The man *who* was here ; *man* is the antecedent.

Who is also applied to inferior animals when spoken of as human beings, in fable; as, The stag *who* came to the river said to himself, etc.

Which is applied to the lower animals and to inanimate things ; as, The horse *which* I bought ; the house *which* I sold.

That is applied to both persons and things, and is used instead of *who* or *which* in certain cases; as, The friend *that* helps ; the bird *that* sings ; the knife *that* cuts.

What includes both the antecedent and the relative, being equivalent to *that which* or *the thing which ;* as, I did *what* he desired me, that is, I did *that which* he desired me.

Who and *which* are thus declined or inflected :—

	SING. AND PLU.	SING. AND PLU.
Nominative,	Who,	Which,
Possessive,	Whose,	Whose,
Objective,	Whom.	Which.

That and *what* are not varied by case.

Who, which, and *what,* when used to ask questions, are called Interrogative Pronouns. When so used, *who* refers to persons, *which* to persons or things out of some definite number, and *what* to persons or things indefinitely ; as, *Who* said so ? *Which* of you said so ? *Which* book shall I take ? *What* person said so ? *What* house is that ?

Ever, compounded with *who, which*, and *what*, form a kind of indefinite relatives; as, *Whoever* expects this; *whichever* way you take; *whatever* is, is right. These are still used by good writers, but whoso, whosoever, whatsoever are obsolete.

What is often used as a simple exclamation, though perhaps forming part of a question; as, *What !* cannot you stay a moment?

DEMONSTRATIVE PRONOUNS

Are so called because they point out particularly the persons or objects to which they refer.

They are *this* and *that*, forming in the plural, *these* and *those*.

This and *these* are applied to persons or things near at hand, or last named; *that* and *those* to persons or things at a distance in time or place; as, *This* earth, *these* trees; *that* sky, *those* stars.

REGULAR AND IRREGULAR VERBS.

Our English Verbs may be divided into two great classes—the Ancient, Strong or Irregular, and the Modern, Weak or Regular.

Trench says:—"The terms 'strong' and 'weak,' in all our grammars, have put out of use the wholly misleading terms, 'irregular' and 'regular.'"

The Ancient, Strong or Irregular Verbs, change the interior vowel in forming the Past Tense, and generally form the Past Participle in *en ;* as, Strike, struck, stricken; fall, fell, fallen. Sometimes they form both the Past Tense and the Participle by modifying the vowel, as, Bite, bit; read, read.

The Modern, Weak or Regular, do *not* change the interior vowel in forming the Past Tense, and they generally form the Past Participle in *d, ed*, or *t ;* as, Move, moved, moved; fill, filled, filled; lose, lost, lost.

All the *Ancient* or Strong Verbs are of Saxon origin.

Many of our Modern or Weak Verbs are derived from the Latin.

There are about one hundred and eighty Strong or Irregular Verbs.

It is not uncommon to hear in the conversation of well-educated people, and to see in otherwise accurately printed works, an erroneous use of the imperfect and perfect forms of some of the irregular verbs; as, *It sunk*, for *it sank*, etc. The following is a list of verbs in which mistakes most frequently occur :—

PRESENT.	PAST.	PERFECT PARTICIPLE.
I begin	I began (not begun)	I have begun
I drink	I drank (not drunk)	I have drunk (not drank)
I lay	I laid	I have laid
I lie	I lay	I have lain (not laid)
I ring	I rang	I have rung (not rang)
I show	I showed	I have shown (not showed)
I shrink	I shrank (not shrunk)	I have shrunk
I sing	I sang (not sung)	I have sung
I sink	I sank (not sunk)	I have sunk
I spring	I sprang (not sprung	I have sprung
I swim	I swam (not swum	I have swum.

SHALL AND WILL.

The perplexities in the use of these words are too common to need any illustrations. A rule by which they may be avoided, however, appears to be still a desideratum. The late Henry Reed, in his posthumous lectures on English literature, reproduces one of the best views of the value and force of these auxiliaries which we have met. He says: "Upon this subject, it has been observed, there is in human nature generally an inclination to avoid speaking presumptuously of the future, in consequence of its awful, irrepressible, and almost instinctive uncertainty, and of our own powerlessness over it, which, in all cultivated languages, has silently and imperceptibly modified the modes of expression with regard to it. Further, there is an instinct of good breeding which leads a man to veil the manifestation of his own will, so as to express himself with becoming modesty. Hence, in the use of these words 'shall' and 'will' (the former associated with compunction, the latter with free volition), we apply them not lawlessly, or at random, but so as to speak submissively in the first person, and courteously when we speak to or of another. This has been a development, but not without a principle in it; for, in our older writers, for instance, in our version of the Bible, 'shall' is applied to all three persons. We had not then reached that stage of politeness which shrinks from even the appearance of speaking compulsorily of another. On the other hand, the Scotch, it is said, use 'will' in the first person ; that is, as a nation, they have not acquired that particular shade of good breeding which shrinks from thrusting itself forward.''

Perhaps the best popular explanation of the general rule may be expressed thus :—

1.		You		shall ;	2.		You		will.
I	} will,	He	}		I	}	shall, He	}	
We		They			We		They		

The form 1, is used to express futurity dependent on the will of the speaker ; as, I *will* pay, You *shall* pay, He *shall* pay.

The form 2, is used to express futurity not dependent on the will of the speaker ; as, I *shall* die, You *will* die, He *will* die.

Originally it is likely that *shall* was always used (as it often is in our translation of the Bible and old books) to express simple futurity ; and *will* to express futurity dependent on the will, not of the speaker but of the person, whether speaker or not. This last use is retained where the *will* is emphatic ; as, He *will* pay, although he is not bound.

It is improper to say, I *will* be hurt if I fall ; because in the first person *will* expresses intention ; now it is not the intention of any person to be hurt. But it is proper to say, You *will* be hurt if you fall, or, He *will* be hurt if he fall ; because in the second and third persons, *will* only foretells or intimates what will happen without implying intention.

It also improper to ask a question in the first person by this verb ; as, *Will* I write ? *Will* we write ? because it is asking what our own will or intention is, which we ought to know better than those whom we ask ; but it is proper to say, *Will* you write ? *Will* he or *will* they write ? for that is asking what their intention is, or what is likely to happen without intention ; as, *Will* the clock strike ?

Shall is used like *will*, in the present tense of the indicative, to express future time, and in the past tense, assertion, referring to a condition which is not fulfilled ; as, I *shall* love ; I *shall* write if you wish.

But with the first person, *shall*, contrary to *will*, expresses in the present tense, mere prediction or foretelling ; and in the past tense mere contingency, without implying any purpose or intention ; with the second or third persons it expresses command or intention in the person speaking ; as, I *shall* be hurt if I fall ; Thou *shalt* not kill. *Shall*, therefore, is used in the first person, singular or plural, both in the present and past tenses, whenever *will* cannot be used for the reasons given. We cannot say, I *will* be afraid, but I *shall* be afraid ; nor, We *will* be hurt if we fall, but We *shall* be hurt if we fall.

ADVERBS,

Like adjectives, are sometimes varied in their endings to express comparison and different degrees of quality. Some adverbs form the comparative and superlative by adding *er* and *est;* as, Soon, soon*er*, soon*est*. Adverbs which end in *ly*, are compared by prefixing *more* and *most;* as, Nobly, *more* nobly, *most* nobly.

A few adverbs are irregular in the formation of the comparative and superlative ; as, Well, better, best.

MISAPPLICATION OF WORDS.

Many persons misapply words, like the foreigner who, looking at a picture of a number of vessels, said, " See what a flock of ships ! " He was told that a flock of ships was called a fleet, and that a fleet of sheep was called a flock. And it was added for his guidance in mastering the intricacies of our language, that a flock of girls is called a bevy, that a bevy of wolves is called a pack, and a pack of thieves is called a gang, and a gang of angels is called a host, and a host of porpoises is called a shoal, and a shoal of buffaloes is called a herd, and a herd of children is called a troop, and a troop of partridges is called a covey, and a covey of beauties is called a galaxy, and a galaxy of ruffians is called a horde, and a horde of rubbish is called a heap, and a heap of oxen is called a drove, and a drove of blackguards is called a mob, and a mob of whales is called a school, and a school of worshippers is called a congregation, and a congregation of engineers is called a corps, and a corps of robbers is called a band, and a band of locusts is called a swarm, and a swarm of people is called a crowd.

DIVISION OF WORDS.

A Syllable is a single sound represented by one or more letters ; as, *a, on, word*.

A syllable always contains at least one vowel.

The number of syllables in a word is always equal to the number of distinct sounds which it contains. Thus the word *strength* contains one distinct sound or syllable; *strength-en* contains two distinct sounds or syllables; *in-ven-tion* contains three; *con-ve-ni-ence,* four; *ver-sa-til-i-ty,* five; *tran-sub-stan-ti-a-tion,* six.

A Word consists of one syllable, or a combination of syllables.

A word of one syllable is called a *Monosyllable,* as, *just;* a word of two syllables, a *Dissyllable,* as, *jus-tice;* a word of three syllables, a *Trisyllable,* as, *jus-ti-fy;* a word of four or more syllables, a *Polysyllable,* as, *jus-ti-fy-ing; jus-ti-fi-ca-tion.*

In writing and printing it is frequently necessary to divide words. Certain rules and cautions must be carefully observed on such occasions.

1. Never divide words of one syllable—*strength, alms, farm.*

2. Never separate letters of the same syllable—*un-speak-able.* Some divide according to pronunciation, but this is objectionable, for words of the same derivation frequently have the accent on different syllables, as, *pre-fer´, pref´-er-ence.*

3. Divide compounds into their component parts—*lamp-post, pen-knife.*

4. Keep the root whole in derivatives—*touch-ing, preach-er, lov-est.*

5. Divide words ending in, *tion, cious, cian, sion,* thus—*mo-tion, vi-cious, mu-si-cian, ex-ten-sion.*

CAPITAL LETTERS

Must be used in the following situations:—for the first letter of

1. The first word of every sentence.

2. The first word of every verse or line of poetry. Every line, as it is commonly called, should be styled a verse, and a series of lines popularly styled a verse is properly called a stanza. A verse is a single measured line, containing a determinate number of syllables, rising and falling, or, in other words, accented and unaccented in a certain prescribed order.

3. The first word of a quotation in a direct form; as, Franklin says : " Serve yourself."

4. All names of the Deity; as, Almighty God, Jehovah, Most High, Jesus Christ, Emmanuel, Our Lord, The Holy Ghost, or Spirit, and He, His, Him, when the Deity is referred to without being named.

5. All proper names, that is, the name of a person, place, etc., and the adjectives derived from proper names; as, His brother Henry speaks German fluently. William the Norman who overcame Harold the Saxon at the battle of Hastings, is styled the Conqueror. The French have landed. Shakespeare was born at Stratford-upon-Avon.

6. All titles of honor; as, the Honorable Oakes Ames; the Reverend Bishop of Oxford; the Chief Justice; the Master of Trinity College.

7. Names of days, months, and holy days; as, Christmas fell on the last Saturday in December. They had a party on New Year's Eve.

8. Any very important word; as, the Revolution, the Union, the Reformation, the Rebellion.

9. The pronoun I, and the interjection O.

If any strong emotion enter into the sentiment, the proper orthography is *Oh*. The aspiration or breathing of the *h* expresses stronger feeling than the mere utterance of the letter O

10. Common nouns personfied; as, "O Death! where is the sting?"

The use of italics in printing is much less frequent than formerly, and the underlining of words in writing, which is used for the same purpose, is now generally discontinued, except in very particular cases.

RULES FOR SPELLING.

Since the time of our earliest authors there has been a gradual improvement and simplification in the spelling of English words, so that the orthography of our language is now very different from what it was at various periods. To a modern reader the spelling of Chaucer and Spenser is as strange as the costume of their age. The tendency to simplify spelling still continues.

A certain degree of uniformity prevails in the spelling of many classes of words; but the exceptions and anomalies are so numerous, that in orthography, as in orthoepy, perfect accuracy is only to be attained by attending to the best authorities.

Bad spelling is always a mark of an imperfect education. But even classical scholars are not always correct in their English orthography. This arises, we believe, from their having mostly learned spelling by the common method of repeating columns of words—a tedious and irksome practice. They never make mistakes in spelling Latin words, because they learn the orthography of that language by constant reading and writing, which are the best methods of acquiring correct spelling in any language. Those whose spelling is incorrect should copy extracts from the best authors, using good editions. The extracts should be copied several times. This practice will not only perfect the orthography but also tend to form a good style of composition. Writing from dictation is an excellent practice, but chiefly useful as a test of spelling, and is not often convenient for adults.

The great number of English words are not reducible to rule, but there are fixed rules for certain formations. The chief rules are the following, and those given for the formation of plurals at page 23 and for the comparison of adjectives at page 28.

1. Words ending in silent *e* drop it before an augment or addition beginning with another vowel, and before *y* when a vowel, that is, when *y* does not begin a word or syllable ; as, Advise, advis-*able*, advis-*ing;* blame, blam-*able*, blam-*ing;* cure, cur-*able*, cur-*ing;* excuse, excus-*able*, excus-*ing;* fame, fam-*ous;* blue, blu-*ish;* rogue, rogu-*ish;* white, whit-*ish;* fence, fenc-*ible;* sense, sens-*ble;* ease, eas-*y;* haste, hast-*y;* paste, past-*y.*

EXCEPTIONS.—The *e* is retained in eye, eye-*ing;* hoe, hoe-*ing;* shoe, shoe-*ing;* tinge, tinge-*ing;* and in dye (to stain), dye-*ing*, to distinguish it from die, dying.

2. Words ending in silent *e* change the *e* into *i* before *fy* and *ty;* as, Active, activ-*i-ty;* cave, cav-*i-ty;* pure, pur-*i-fy.*

EXCEPTIONS.—Safe-ty ; sure-ty.

3. Words ending in silent *e* generally retain it before *ful, less, ly, ment, some,* and *ty;* as, Waste, waste-*ful;* guile, guile-*less;* brave, brave-*ly;* abridge, abridge-*ment;* move, move-*ment;* acknowledge, acknowledge-*ment;* wholesome, wholesome-*ness.*

EXCEPTIONS.—Argue, argument; awe, awful; due, duly; true, truly; whole, wholly.

Smart says:—"*Judgement,acknowledgement,* etc., are less frequently spelled without the *e* after *g* than with it. If so spelled, the *g* is irregular in sound, being never elsewhere soft but when *e, i,* or *y* follows. Johnson, who spells the other words without the *e,* spells judgement with it. Todd, in his edition of Johnson, makes all these words consistent, and all regular in spelling." In this particular Smart follows Todd.

Mr. Thomas Ford says :—" The probable accidental omission of the *e* in the words *abridgment, acknowledgment,* and *judgment,* in the original edition of Johnson's Dictionary, have given a precedent for long-continued deviations for the rule which preserves that vowel from elision in the above words, and which would appear to be the same as that guiding its preservation when *c* or *g* comes soft before words terminating with *able*. There is no apparent reason for the omission of the *e* in these three words, more than in others of the same class or formation, and, indeed, they are now frequently spelled with that vowel. Although the *e* was omitted in the original edition of Johnson's Dictionary, it was restored in that by Todd. Dr. Lowth and Mr. Walker are of opinion that the silent *e* in such words ought to be preserved."

4. Words ending in silent *e*, preceded by *c* or *g* soft, retain *e* before *able* and *ous ;* as, Charge, charg*eable ;* change, chang*eable ;* manage, manag*eable ;* peace, peac*eable ;* service, servic*eable ;* courage, courag*eous ;* outrage, outrag*eous.*

Exceptions.—Grac*e* and vic*e* change the *e* into *i ;* as, Grac*i*ous, vic*i*ous.

5. Words ending in silent *e*, preceded by *c* or *g* soft, drop the *e* before *ing ;* as, Abridg*e*, abridg-*ing ;* alleg*e*, alleg-*ing ;* enclose, enclos-*ing ;* judg*e*, judg-*ing ;* lodg*e*, lodg-*ing ;* pronounce, pronouncing *;* state, stat-*ing.*

6. Words in which silent *e* is preceded by *l, m, s,* or *v*, and followed by *able,* are unsettled, some authorities dropping the *e* while others retain it. Webster omits it, and consistency is in favor of his orthography—Movable, blamable, provable, etc.

Walker says :—" The mute *e* ought to have no place, when followed by a vowel, in words of our own composition, where the preceding vowel has its general sound; and therefore, as it is *inclinable, desirable,* etc., so it ought to be *reconcilable, reconcilably,* etc. This was the orthography adopted by Dyche, before it became so fashionable to imitate the French."

7. Words ending in *ie* change those vowels into *y* before *ing,* without exception; as, Beli*e*, beli*e*d, bely-*ing ;* di*e*, di*e*d, dy-*ing ;* hi*e*, hi*e*d, hy-*ing ;* li*e*, li*e*d, ly-*ing ;* outli*e*, outlain, outly-*ing ;* outvi*e*, outvi*e*d, outvy-*ing ;* ti*e*, ti*e*d, ty-*ing.*

8. Words ending in *y* after a consonant, change the *y* into *i* before all augments, except *ing, ish,* and *s* preceded by an apostrophe for the possessive case; as, Fancy, fanc*iful ;* saucy, sauc*i-ness ;*

merry, merrier, merriest ; Fancy-ing ; study-ing ; baby-ish ; dry-ish ; beauty's charm ; fancy's beam.

EXCEPTIONS.—Beauteous, duteous, bounteous.

Dryly, dryness, shyly, shyness, slyly slyness, and some others, are considered to be exceptions. It were better that these words conformed to the rule, and changed the y into i, but custom, which is all-powerful, forbids it.

9. Words ending in y after a vowel do not change the y before an augment ; as, Delay, delay-ed, delay-ing ; obey, obey-ed, obey-ing ; convey, convey-ed, convey-ing ; joy, joy-ous.

EXCEPTIONS.—Day, daily; lay, laid; pay paid; say, said ; stay staid.

10. Words of one syllable ending in a single consonant preceded by a single vowel, double the consonant before a vowel augment ; as, Bog, bog-gy ; fog, fog-gy ; gum, gum-my ; mud, mud-dy ; knot, knot-ty ; pup, pup-py ; star, star-ry.

11. Words of one syllable having two final consonants, or the final consonant preceded by two vowels, do not double the final consonant ; as, Ash, ash-y ; cloud, clou-dy ; chalk, chalk-y ; cool, cool-est ; dusk, dusk-y ; hill, hill-y ; meek, meek-er ; stern, stern-est.

12. Words of more than one syllable, accented on the final syllable, ending in a single consonant, preceded by a single vowel, double the final consonant before a vowel augment ; as, Refer', refer-red, refer-ring ; enrol', enrol-led, enrol-ling ; prefer', prefer-red, prefer-ring. The consonant is not doubled before an augment beginning with another consonant ; as, prefer-ment; enrol-ment. Pref'erence and ref'erence having the accent transferred to the first syllable, do not double the r.

13. Words of the above class, not accented on the final syllable, or if accented on the final syllable, having the single final consonant preceded by a diphthong, do not double the final consonant ; as, Cov'et ; covet-ed, covet-ing ; cred'it, credit-ed, credit-ing ; lim'it, limit-ed, limit-ing ; conceal', conceal-ing, conceal-ment ; reveal, reveal-ing.

There has long been much uncertainty as to the propriety of doubling the final consonant of words before adding the augments ed, er, or ing, and as these augmented words are seldom inserted in our dictionaries, great confusion upon this subject is common. The rules for the doubling of the consonants before these augments is generally known and practised but not universally, and it has not yet become the custom to spell *coun'sellor, le'veller, wor'-shipper*, etc., with one *l* or *p* only, although these and words of the same class are occasionally written and printed with their respective final consonants single when followed by augments. Lowth, Webster, and other eminent authorities have observed that the doubling of these consonants is as anomaly in spelling which neither analogy nor pronunciation justifies.

Walker says:—" The letter *l*, has not only, like *f* and *s*, the privilege of doubling itself at the end of a word, but it has an exclusive privilege of being double where they remain single. Thus, according to the general rule, when a verb ends in a single consonant, preceded by a single vowel, and the accent is on the last syllable, the consonant is doubled when a participial termination is added, as, *abet, abetted, beg, begging, begin, beginning,* etc.; but when the accent is *not* on the last syllable of the verb, the consonant remains single, as *suffered, suffering, benefiting,* etc., but the *l* is doubled whether the accent be on the last syllable or not, as, *dwelling, levelling, victualling, travelling, traveller,* etc."

Although it must be admitted that the doubling of the *l* and *p* in words not accented on the final syllable, is against all rule, and only used to satisfy the eye which has become accustomed to it, we give a list of words in which all-powerful custom incorrectly requires their use.

Apparel, apparelled, apparelling.

Barrel, barrelled, barrelling; Bevel, bevelled, bevelling.

Cancel, cancellated, cancellation, cancelled, cancelling; Carol, carolled, carolling; Counsel, counsellable, counselled, counsellor, counselling; Cudgel, cudgelled, cudgeller, cudgelling.

Dial, dialled, dialling, diallist; Dishevel, dishevelled, dishevelling; Drivel, drivelled, driveller, drivelling; Duel, dueller, duelling, duellist, duello.

Embowel, embowelled, embowelling; Enamel, enamelled, enameller, enamelling.

Flannel, flannelled, flannelling; Fuel, fuelled, fuelling.

Gambol, gambolled, gambolling; Gospel, gospelled, gospeller, gospelling; Gravel, gravelled, gravelling; Grovel, grovelled, groveller, grovelling.

Handsel, handselled, handselling.

Jewel, jewelled, jeweller, jewelling, jewellery.

Kennel, kennelled, kennelling.

Label, labelled, labelling; Level, levelled, leveller, levelling (levelness); Libel, libelled, libeller, libelling, libellous.

Marshal, marshalled, marshalling; Marvel, marvelled, marvelling, marvellous.

Outrival, outrivalled, outrivalling.

Panel, panelled, panelling; Parcel, parcelled, parceller, parcelling; Pencil, pencilled, pencilling; Peril, perilled, perilling (perilous); Pommel, pommelled, pommelling.

Quarrel, quarrelled quarrelling.

Ravel, ravelled, ravelling; Revel (revelry), revelled, reveller, revelling; Rival, rivalry, rivalled, rivalling.

Shovel, shovelled, shovelling; Shrivel, shrivelled, shrivelling, shriveller; Snivel, sniveller, snivelled, snivelling.

Tinsel, tinselled, tinselling; Trammel, trammelled, trammelling; Travel, travelled, traveller, travelling; Trowel, trowelled, trowelling; Tunnel, tunnelled, tunnelling.

Worship, worshipped, worshipper, worshipping.

14. Words ending in any double letter except *l*, retain the double letter before the augments *ful, ly, less,* and *ness ;* as, Bliss, bliss*ful ;* cross, cross-*ly ;* gross, gross-*ly ;* success, success-*less ;* care*less*, careless-*ness ;* gruff, gruff-*ness*.

15. Words ending in *ll* drop one *l* before *ful, ly,* and *less ;* as, Ski*ll*, ski*lful ;* fu*ll*, fu*l-ly ;* ski*ll*, ski*l-less*.

16. Words ending in *ll* retain the double letter before the augment *ness ;* as, I*ll*, i*ll-ness ;* sma*ll*, sma*ll-ness ;* ta*ll*, ta*ll-ness*.

EXCEPTIONS.—Chilness, dulness, fulness. These are excepted by all authorities, but many other words of this class are spelled differently in various dictionaries. Webster doubles the *l*, and consistency is in favor of his orthography. Walker says that if *tallness* is deprived of one *l* it ought undoubtedly to be pronounced like the first syllable of *tal-low*, which sufficiently shows the necessity of spelling it with double *l*. He also says :—"As *ll* is a mark of the deep, broad sound of *a* in ball, tall, etc , so the same letters are the sign of the long open sound of *o* in boll (a round stalk of a plant), to joll, noll (the head), knoll (a little hill), poll, roll, scroll, droll, troll, stroll, toll ; for which reason leaving out one *l* is an omission of the utmost importance to the sound of the words ; for, as the pronunciation sometimes alters the spelling, so the spelling sometimes alters the pronunciation."

17. Words ending in *l* or *ll*, both as simples and compounds, are

still unsettled. Webster doubles the *l*, and we think his rule should be followed.

He says:—"The omission of one *l* in befall, install, recall, enthrall, etc., is by no means to be vindicated; as by custom the two letters *ll* serve as a guide to the true pronunciation, that of broad *a* or *aw*. It is therefore expedient to retain both letters."

Churchill says:—"That some regular principle on this head should be adopted, is desirable. Uniformity to retain the double letter would be simple and easy."

EXCEPTIONS.—Almighty, always, fulfil, welcome.

18. Words augmented by *full*, generally drop one *l* when nouns and always when adjectives; as,

Armful, glassful, handful, pailful, spoonful, etc.

Awful, blissful, brimful, careful, cheerful, etc.

When the augment *ly* is required, the *l* is doubled; as, Awful-*ly*; blissful-*ly*; playful-*ly*; useful-*ly*, etc.

19. Words ending in two consonants never double the last before the augments *ed* and *ing*; as, Abstract, abstracted, abstracting; attest, attested, attesting; correct, corrected, correcting; object, objected, objecting; pervert, perverted, perverting.

A SHORT SYNTAX.

When several nouns are joined together, some of which require *a* before them and others *an*, the indefinite article should be repeated before each of them; as, *A* horse, *an* ass, and *a* cow.

When two or more nouns or adjectives are joined together, the article is placed only before the first of them, if they are applied to the same person or thing; as, *The* great and good Alfred.

But it should be placed before each of them if they are applied to different persons or things; as, *The* English and *the* French people.

An article should be placed before a participle used as a noun and followed by *of*; as, *In the hearing of* the judge. But it is incorrect to say, "Let us guard against *the giving* way to resentment," because the participle, not admitting *of* after it, to govern the noun following, is simply a verb, and therefore the article should be omitted.

The omission of the article before the limiting words, *few*, *little*, and *small*, increases the restriction. I used *little* severity, means not much and may imply none ; but, I used *a little* severity, implies some and perhaps much.

When the possessor is described by two or more nouns, the apostrophe, or sign of the possessive case, should be placed after the last noun ; as, In William the *Conqueror's* time.

When the thing possessed belongs to two or more nouns, the sign of the possessive should be put after each ; as, It was my *father's, brother's*, and *grand-father's* estate.

The objective case with *of* is frequently used instead of the possessive ; as, The servant *of* my *father.*

But when the thing is only one of a number belonging to the possessor, both the possessive case and *of* are used ; as, A servant *of* my *father's,* the word *servant* being understood after *father's ;* the full construction of the phrase being, " A servant *out of*," or "*from among* my father's servants."

The verb *to be* should have the same case after it as came before it ; as, *It* is *I* (not *me*), be not afraid ; *who* (not *whom*) do men say that *I* am ? *Whom* (not *who*) do they represent *me* to be ?

A noun or pronoun which answers a question, should be in the same case with the noun or pronoun which asks the question ; as, Who said that?—*He*, not him ; *who* is there ?—*I*, not *me ; whom* did you see ?—*Him ; whose* house is this ?—*John's.*

A noun or pronoun following *than* or *as*, must be of the same case as that with which the comparison is made, though not immediately connected ; as, *I* am as old *as he* (is) ; *he* is richer *than I* (am) ; he praised *them* more *than me.*

The indefinite pronouns *all, any, none, such*, etc., require the verbs to be in the singular or plural, according to the sense to be conveyed ; as, *All* (everything) *is* peaceful ; *all* (people) *are* offended with you ; *is* there *any* ale in the house ? My right there *is none* (no one) to dispute ; I wanted some apples but there *were none* (not any)

Two or more nouns in the singular number, separated by *or* or *nor* require the verb to be in the singular ; as, Either John *or* Thomas speaks ; Neither John *nor* Thomas *was* present. The reason of this obviously is that only one of them is said to speak, not both ; and that the not being present is affirmed of John and Thomas separately, not together.

Two or more nouns in the singular number, joined by the conjunction *and,* require the verb to be in the plural number ; as, John and Thomas *are* present.

When two nouns, or a noun and pronoun, in the singular number are connected by the preposition *with,* or by such expressions as, *as well as,* the verb must be in the singular ; as, John *with* his son *was* in town to-day ; he *as well as* his son *is* in town.

When two or more nominatives in different numbers are joined by *or* or *nor,* the verb must be in the plural ; as, Either *you* or *I are* in fault ; neither *cucumbers* nor *vinegar are* to be had.

The plural nominative must always be placed next to the verb ; as, *Are* the *people* or the King to blame ?

When two or more nominatives in the same number, but of different persons, are joined by *or* or *nor,* the verb agrees with the last ; as, Either thou or *he is* wrong.

When two or more nominatives of different persons are joined by the conjunction *and,* the verb agrees with the first person in preference to the second, and with the second in preference to the third ; as, You and *I have* done our duty ; *you* and he *have* had *your* share.

Collective nouns should be followed by verbs in the singular or in the plural number, according as unity or plurality of idea is to be expressed ; as, The council *is* sitting ; the clergy *are* divided among themselves. D'Orsey says :—" Usage, which gives law to language, is here quite at fault, our best authors being inconsistent with themselves, and with each other. Till certain rules shall be established, the following are offered as approximating to fixed principles :—

" If a collective noun is preceded by *a* or *an,* and expresses a *vague* number or quantity, the verb is generally plural ; as, A *number* of men *go* out to hunt.

" If a collective noun marks a complete or determinate number, and is preceded by such defining terms as *the, this, that, my, thy, his, each, every, no,* etc., the verb is singular ; as, The *number increases* daily ; my *class improves ;* no *tribe appears* more savage.

" In the case of such words as *committee, council, society, public, majority, minority,* etc., the verb should be singular if the statement is true only of the whole body ; but plural if what is asserted applies rather to the individuals ; *Congress has* determined ; the *committee were* divided in their opinions.

" Such terms as *couple, dozen, score, million,* etc., expressing a known number in the singular form, require plural verbs. *Pair*, however, takes the singular. There *were* a *dozen*, but there *is* a *pair*.

"Such expressions as the following are wrong :—*Those sort* of people do injury; *these kind* of oranges are bitter. Yet there is something very harsh in the change to the singular; as, *That sort* of people *does* injury; *this kind* of oranges *is* bitter. It is better to transpose the order, and retain the plural verb, thus : *People* of that sort do injury; *oranges* of this kind *are* bitter."

The verb *to be* is often preceded by *it*, used as a sort of impersonal nominative, in which case the singular number is used, though followed by a plural noun; as, *It is* six weeks ago; *It is James and John* who are wrong.

. The adverb *there* is often employed in a similar manner, but it allows the verb to agree with the noun following it; as, *There are apples* on the tree.

A singular verb, however, is used when it is introduced by this or any other adverb, and followed by two or more singular nouns as, There *is* a knife and fork on the table.

D'Orsey says :—"It would be insufferably harsh, however it might be contended for as correct grammar, to say, ' There *are* a knife and fork.' It must be, ' There *is*,' which may be justified by supposing that an ellipsis is used, and that the full expression is, ' There is a knife, and there is a fork.' The necessity of using the singular verb will more fully appear if we suppose a pronoun used in the sentence, ' Bring me a knife and fork; there is *one* on the table.' We feel it to be impossible to use any plural pronoun to stand for knife and fork in this case. In like manner we would set down as a pedant the man who should ask, ' Where *are* my hat and stick ? ' The reason appears to be, that the sense is complete with the first nominative, and the ear has been offended by the plural verb before the second nominative is announced to account for it. It is otherwise when the sense is suspended, as it is by the use of auxiliaries, ' Where *have* my hat and stick been put ? ' Here the mind is carried forward to *been put*, as the completion of *have*, and the two nominatives have appeared in the meantime."

The present infinitive, and not the perfect tense, should be used after a past tense; as, I intended to *see* you, not *to have seen* you; unless we speak of something prior to the time indicated in the past tense; as, He *appeared to have seen* better days. The past, and not the pluperfect tense, should be used in the potential mood; as, I thought he *would* die, not *would have* died.

The adverbs *hence, thence,* and *whence* do not require *from* before them, as each contains in itself the power of that preposition; as Depart *hence,* that is, *from this place; Whence* came you? that is, *from what place;* He went *thence,* that is, *from that place.*

When a preposition governs the relative *who* or *which,* it must be placed before it, and both must precede the verb; as, *To whom* do you speak? not, *who* (or *whom*) do you speak *to?* The man to *whom* I spoke.

Yet when the pronoun is suppressed, the preposition is put after the verb; as, The man I spoke *to* yesterday.

The relative *that* is not subject to this rule; as, It is the same horse *that* you were looking *at.*

* Certain words and phrases require certain prepositions to be used with them. Some admit different prepositions for different meanings; thus, You are disappointed *of* a thing which you expected, *if* you do not obtain it; you are disappointed *in* it, if you obtain it and it does not answer your expectations. The prepositions proper to be used in each case must be learned not by rules, but by reading the best authors, and carefully considering the logical meaning of those which you use.

Some conjunctions have corresponding conjunctions, by which they should be followed; thus, *both* is followed by *and; either* by *or; neither* by *nor; though* by *yet; whether* by *or,* etc.; as, *Both* you *and* I saw it; *either* you *or* I must go; *neither* you *nor* I saw him; *though* he was rich, *yet* for our sakes he became poor. *As, as* is used in affirmative, but *so, as* in negative comparison; as, Mine is *as* good *as* yours; but his is not *so* good *as* either.

PUNCTUATION

Is the art of dividing a written composition into sentences or parts of sentences, by points or stops, for the purpose of marking, to the eye, the different pauses which the grammatical construction requires. Much confusion has been caused by confounding the Elocutionary Pause with the Grammatical Point. The two are distinct—pauses belonging to the expression and meaning of a sentence, and points to its meaning and construction. The punctuation is usually made by the printer, according to the rule which he prefers. These rules differ greatly, many being arbitary and illogical, and others unsettled. Few authors have a correct knowledge of punctuation, and many consider the subject beneath their serious attention. Because they know what they mean to express (which, by the by, is not always the case), they are apt to think the reader will, as readily as themselves, understand their meaning. They suffer for this neglect by many of their finest thoughts being but imperfectly understood and appreciated. Some writers seem to throw in their commas, semicolons, etc., promiscuously ; while others scarcely use a point in a sentence. Others, again, have very extraordinary crotchets upon punctuation, and will not allow a printer's reader (who is usually an excellent grammarian) to alter a single comma, or improve the construction of a sentence, however awkwardly put together.

Of late years, a system of punctuation styled high pointing has been adopted by many authors. It seems to consist in a superabundant use of the comma, this point being placed wherever there is the slightest opportunity for making a pause in reading the words aloud. The system of high pointing has, doubtless, arisen from writers confounding the grammatical points with the elocutionary pauses. They have punctuated their writings as they would have read them aloud, not perceiving that few works, in proportions to the numbers written, are read aloud ; and also, that it would be difficult to express by marks all the pauses made by a good reader or speaker ; still more difficult to express by marks the duration of those pauses ; and that such marks would be unsightly in print, and beget a mechanical mode of delivery. The *points* are intended for the *eyes* of the reader, to make the sense of the words clear to him at sight. The *pauses* made by a person reading aloud, or by a good speaker, are not only used to make the sense clear to the hearer, but also to produce many very striking and expressive effects, and to give the reader time to take breath, and an occasional rest.

Correct punctuation is most important to the sense. A passage wrongly punctuated may be made to bear a meaning totally different to that which the writer intended to convey, as the following example will prove.

When Lady Macbeth snatches the daggers from the hands of her husband, and goes to the chamber of the murdered Duncan, to " to smear the sleepy grooms with blood," so that " it may seem

their guilt," Macbeth, left alone, in the agony of his remorse thus
apostrophizes his crimsoned hands. The last verse of this magni-
ficent passage is here pointed as it was given, probable from the
time of the Restoration until Garrick hit upon the right pause:—

> " Whence is that knocking ?
> How is't with me, when every noise appals me ?
> What hands are here ? Ha! they pluck out mine eyes !
> Will all great Neptune's ocean wash this blood
> Clean from my hand ? No ; this my hand will rather
> The multitudinous seas incarnadine,
> Making the green one, red."

Now, to call the ocean " the green one " is to convey a very ludicrous meaning; but by placing a dash after "green," as Garrick
did, a sublime idea is expressed, Macbeth being made to explain
that his bloody hands would redden the entire ocean:—

> " No ; this my hand will rather
> The multitudinous seas incarnadine,
> Making the green—one red."

It has indeed been truly said that there is but one step from the
sublime to the ridiculous. That step may be made by a point
falsely placed. The necessity of punctuation may be illustrated
by the following verses :—

> I saw a peacock with a fiery tail
> I saw a blazing star that dropp'd down hail
> I saw a cloud begirt with ivy round
> I saw a sturdy oak creep on the ground
> I saw a daisy swallow up a whale
> I saw the brackish sea brimful of ale
> I saw a phial-glass sixteen yards deep
> I saw a well full of men's tears to weep
> I saw man's eyes all on a flame of fire
> I saw a house high as the moon or higher
> I saw the radiant sun at deep midnight
> I saw the man who saw.this dreadful sight

Which should be punctuated thus :—

> I saw a peacock; with a fiery tail
> I saw a blazing star; that dropped down hail
> I saw a cloud; begirt with ivy round
> I saw a sturdy oak; creep on the ground

I saw a daisy ; swallow up a whale
I saw the brackish sea ; brimful of ale
I saw a phial-glass ; sixteen yards deep
I saw a well ; full of men's tears to weep
I saw man's eyes ; all on a flame of fire
I saw a house ; high as the moon or higher
I saw the radiant sun ; at deep midnight
I saw the man who saw this dreadful sight.

The points used to mark the grammatical structure of sentences are the comma (,), the semicolon (;), the colon (:), the period, or full stop (.), the note of interrogation (?), the note of exclamation (!), the dash (—), the apostrophe ('), the parenthesis (), the hyphen (-), and quotation marks (" " ' ').

The following are the chief rules for correct punctuation :—

THE COMMA

Is used to group words into clauses, to mark parenthetical clauses ·and to show an ellipsis or omission of some word or words.

A comma should be placed wherever there is an ellipsis, or omission of a word.

When several words of the same class follow one another, without conjunctions, commas should be placed between them ; as, It is the duty of a friend to advise, comfort, exhort. Reputation, virtue, happiness greatly depend upon the choice of companions.

There is considerable difference of opinion as to whether words situated like the preceding should be pointed off from those to which they are mutually related, as well as from each other. " It seems to be admitted, that if adjectives or adverbs, they should not be separated from the words they qualify ; as, A learned, wise, and good man ; correctly, perspicuously, and elegantly written. But when they are nominatives belonging to the same verb, or verbs governing the same objective, some authors place a comma after them ; as, Self-conceit, presumption, and obstinacy, blast the prospect of many a youth.

> To guide, to cheer, to charm, to bless,
> To sanctify, our pilgrimage on earth.

While others would omit the commas after *obstinacy* or *sanctify ;* and as the tendency at present is to the use of much fewer stops than formerly, we are disposed to justify the omission."

But there is a much better reason for omitting the comma. In the first example there is an ellipsis of *and* and *blast*, etc., after *self-conceit*, and an ellipsis of *blast*, etc., but not of *and* after *presumption* and in each place a comma is required to show the place of the ellipsis; but there is not any at *obstinacy*, and consequently a comma is not needed. In the second example there is an ellipsis of *our pilgrimage*, etc., after each of the verbs except *sanctify*, and consequently a comma should be placed after each verb except *sanctify*

When words of the same class follow each other in pairs, a comma should be placed between each pair; as, Truth is fair and artless, simple and sincere, uniform and constant.

The clauses of a compound sentence should be separated by commas; as, He studies diligently, and makes great progress.

Words denoting the person or object addressed, and words placed in opposition, are separated by commas; as, My son, give me thy heart. The butterfly, child of the summer, flutters in the sun.

Words which express contrast or opposition, should be separated by a comma, whether connected by a conjunction or not; as, He was learned, but not pedantic. Though deep, yet clear; though gentle, yet not dull. The flock, and not the fleece, ought to be the object of the shepherd's care.

Adverbial and modifying words and phrases should be separated by commas; as, Finally, let me repeat what I stated before.

An expression, supposed to be spoken, or taken from another writer, but not formally quoted, should be preceded by a comma; as, I say unto all, Watch. Plutarch calls lying, the vice of slaves.

A word or phrase emphatically repeated should be separated by a comma; as, Turn ye, turn ye, why will ye die ?

Phrases formed of one or more adverbs, with participles, infinitives, or nouns with prepositions, should be separated from the other phrases by commas; as, I shall not, *however*, dispute his right. It proceeded, *in a great degree, if not altogether*, from misapprehension.

When, however, an adverb does not appear as a phrase, but directly qualifies some word in the sentence, it must not be separated by a comma. Parenthetical clauses should have commas before and after them.

If we say: "The diligent student will most certainly excel," there occur here no words but what belong grammatically to each other, and stand in their natural order; but if we say : "The diligent student, it it certain, will excel," the words, *it is certain*, having no grammatical relation to those either before or after them, form a parenthetical clause, which requires to be marked off.

THE SEMICOLON

Is used to separate those divisions of a sentence called members, which are larger than phrases.

When a sentence consists of two parts, the one complete in itself, and the other added as an inference, or to give some explanation, they are separated by a semicolon; as, Economy is no disgrace ; for it is better to live on a little than to outlive a great deal. I have no respect for titled rank, unless it be accompanied by true nobility of soul; but I have remarked in all countries where artificial distinctions exist that the very highest classes are always the most courteous and unassuming.

When a sentence contains an enumeration of several particulars, the clauses should be separated by semicolons : as, Philosophers assert that nature is unlimited in her operations; that she has inexhaustible treasures in reserve ; that knowledge is progressive ; and that all future generations will continue to make discoveries, of which we have not the slightest idea.

When several distinct facts or augments are grouped together, and made constructionally to correspond with each other, they should be separated by semicolons : as, Our business is interrupted ; our repose is troubled ; our pleasures are saddened ; our very studies are poisoned and perverted; and knowledge is rendered worse than ignorance.

THE COLON

Is used to mark a greater division of a sentence than that requiring a semicolon.

When a sentence consists of two parts, the one complete in itself, and the other containing an additional remark, the sense but not the construction of which depends on the former, they should be separated by a colon; as, Study to acquire the habit of thinking: no study is more important.

Whether a colon or a semicolon should be used sometimes depends on the insertion or omission of a conjunction; as, Do not flatter yourself with the hope of perfect happiness: there is no such thing in the world. Do not flatter yourself with the hope of perfect happiness; for there is no such thing in the world.

When the sense of several members of a sentence, which are separated from each other by semicolons, depends on the last clause, that clause should be separated from the others by a colon; as, A Divine legislator, uttering his voice from heaven; an Almighty governor, stretching forth his arm to reward or punish: these are considerations which overawe the world, support integrity, and check guilt.

The colon is used after an independent prefatory passage introducing a speech or quotation; as, Eustace St. Pierre thus addressed the assembly: "My friends, we are brought to great straights this day."

It is also used to mark the introduction of the several heads into which a subject is divided; and specifications of any kind.

THE PERIOD, OR FULL STOP

Is used to mark the end of all sentences, unless they are interrogative or exclamatory, in which cases the notes of interrogation or exclamation must be used.

Care should be taken not to divide a sentence into sentences instead of marking the divisions by semicolons; as, His understanding, acute and vigorous, was well fitted for diving into the human mind. His humor, lively and versatile, could paint justly and agreeably what he saw. He possessed a rapid and clear conception with an animated and graceful style. Semicolons should be used instead of periods at *mind* and *saw*, and the last member be connected by *and*.

The period is also used to mark abbreviations and contractions; as, M. C., Member of Congress; Esq., for Esquire; Co., for Company, etc.

Abbreviations should be kept for special uses in lists of catalogues, etc., and avoided as much as possible in every kind of elegant or polite composition.

Whenever abbreviations are used, they should be followed by the period to denote that they are abbreviations, and in positions where a comma, semicolon, or colon would be necessary after the full word, it must be attached to the abbreviations; as, F. A. A., M. C. When a sentence finishes with an abbreviation, there is no necessity for a second period.

The note of interrogation is used after sentences which ask questions; as, Whence comest thou? It must be placed after every distinct question, even though several should occur in succession. It must not be used after words which merely state that a question has been asked; as, An infidel once conversing with a Christian, asked him what his God was, and how large he was.

The Spaniards place the note of interrogation at the commencement of the sentence which contains the question, to prepare the reader for the question which the sentence puts.

The note of exclamation is used after all interjections, and after words or sentences which express emotion, admiration, etc.; as, Hark! he comes. O Peace! how desirable thou art!

When these feelings are expressed in an interrogative form, and no answer is either expected or implied, the note of exclamation should be used instead of the note of interrogation.

The note of exclamation should be carefully and sparingly used.

The dash is used to mark a break or abrupt turn in a sentence; as,

Here lies the great—False marble, where?
Nothing but sordid dust lies here.

Also when a word is repeated with explanation; to supply the place of suppressed letters or words; after the side-heading of paragraphs; between an extract or quotation and the author's name, if the latter be added; and in place of the preposition *to;* as, Page 10—20.

The parenthesis is used to enclose an explanatory clause or member of a sentence, not absolutely necessary to the sense; as,

Know then this truth (enough for man to know),
Virtue alone is happiness below.

The hyphen (-) is used to connect compound words. But many are now written without the hyphen, chiefly those composed of two nouns, as *milkmaid*, etc. It was formerly used to separate a prefix from the root, but it is not so used now; unless the omission of it would produce a double vowel or two vowels that might be mistaken for a proper diphthong. Thus we write *coequal* and *coincide* ; but *co-operate* and *re-enter* are preferable to *cooperate* and *reenter*.

The hyphen is also used at the end of a line when a word is divided for want of space.

GRAMMAR MADE EASY.

A VERY INTERESTING BOOK

On a Proverbially Dry and Uninteresting Subject.

The author has, with a tact and skill which shows him to be a thorough master of the subject, stripped the language of all unnecessary verbiage and gone right to the point, and used such matter only that is absolutely needed. It is, in fact, the golden grains of Grammar, sifted from the useless mass of chaff that it is usually invested with. The book is especially adapted for those who have arrived to years of understanding, but who have never had the opportunity of acquiring grammatical knowledge, and also for those who have, in early years, had some knowledge of it, but who have neglected or forgotten to practice it. By a perusal of this small manual, a person gets, with small effort, that which takes with the ordinary Grammars now in use, months of dry, tedious drudgery to get anything like a fair knowledge of the English language.

It is a complete Manual of Instruction for Correct Speaking, Writing, and Spelling, for Adults.

PRICE 20 CENTS.

HOW TO BE AN ORATOR.

At no period of our country's history was public speaking more in demand than at the present time. The speaker everywhere is welcomed, and his calling honored. A man, however extensive his knowledge, or brilliant his attainments, if he has not the power of communicating them in public, is doomed to mediocrity, and ofttimes obscurity, whilst a man with moderate attainments, who has cultivated the art of public speaking, will always be a man of influence, and looked upon as an authority on any point at issue. New questions are arising every day, relating to Politics, Social and Sanitary matters and morals, which, unless their true meaning and importance are placed before the people, will cause much trouble in the future, and even threaten the safety of our republican institutions. The Book gives complete directions for composing a speech, illustrated by the various kinds of oratory. It should be in the hands of every person who is desirous of becoming proficient in the supremely useful and noble art of oratory.

CONTENTS.

Importance of the Orator—Power of the Orator—Various Kinds of Oratory—Prepared Speech—Constructing a Speech—Short Speeches—Command of Language—Reading and Thinking—Style—Hasty Composition—Forming a Style—Copiousness and Preciseness—Diction and Specific Terms—Variety of Language—Too Great Care About Words—Epithets—Precision—Synonyms—Perspicuity—Long and Short Sentences—Tropes and Figures—Metaphor—Simile, etc., etc.

The instruction given will enable any one to appear with dignity and distinction before any audience.

PRICE 15 CENTS.

☞ *Sent by mail, to any address, on receipt of price.*

HOW TO
SPEAK AND WRITE
WITH
ELEGANCE AND EASE.

A valuable little Manual for the use of Readers, Writers, and Talkers. It shows the most prevalent errors that the inexperienced fall into. The examples are made extremely plain and clear. In every case the correct forms are given. It should be the companion of every person, young or old, who desires to Speak, Write, or Read with Precision and Correctness.

PRICE 15 CENTS.

HOW TO PRONOUNCE
DIFFICULT WORDS.

There are few persons who have not, at times, been in doubt respecting the true pronunciation of a word they desired to use. Even those who have had the advantages of a liberal education are frequently confused and confounded by uncertainty of the correct sounding of words they need to express their views. This uncertainty can now be avoided. By the aid of this book the hardest words or most difficult terms in the English language can be pronounced with absolute ease and accuracy. It contains also much useful information relating to the choice of words, and gives rules for pronouncing French, Italian, German, Russian, Danish, Norwegian, and other foreign words that are constantly occurring in the current literature of the day.

PRICE 15 CENTS.

SLANG AND VULGAR
PHRASES AND FORMS.

A COLLECTION OF
Objectional Words, Inaccurate Terms, Barbarisms, Colloquisms, Quaint Expressions, Cant Phrases, Provincialisms, Perversions and Misapplication of Terms,

As used in the various States of the Union.

As a Dictionary of local peculiarities and State idiosyncrasies it is a curiosity, and deserves a place in every library. The whole collection is arranged, explained and corrected.

PRICE 15 CENTS.

Sent by mail, to any address, on receipt of price.

A SCIENTIFIC TREATISE

ON

STAMMERING

AND

STUTTERING,

AND ITS CURE.

We have here this difficult subject treated so intelligently and plainly that any person interested can read and learn the causes of the peculiar and distressing impediment in his speech—why it is that he can speak some words plainly and easily, and others not at all—why it is that some stammerers can speak fluently words beginning with B, P, Sp, etc., and cannot utter words beginning with C, K, Q, etc.—why it is that one day he can converse quite well, and on another can talk only with great hesitation and difficulty. In short, it thoroughly explains the different causes that produce stammering, and then proceeds to make plain the means of cure, so that any person with a determination to succeed, by following the instructions given, can cure himself of this most unhappy affliction, and at no expense but the cost of the book. In parts II and III are given all the secret and "instant" Cures—averaging in price from $10 to $75—such as are practiced by the "professional" curers of stammering. Therefore, possessing this little work, you possess a full knowledge of the causes of stammering, and all that is known for its prompt and permanent removal. Of the value of this work we have received some very gratifying letters of commendation, from those who have found cures for themselves in its pages, and which would be given here did space permit.

Beautifully printed on toned paper; English Cloth, Beveled Boards, making a very handsome volume.

PRICE $1.25.

☞ *Sent by mail, to any address, on receipt of price.*

THE AMATEUR PAINTER.

A MANUAL OF INSTUCTION IN THE ARTS OF

PAINTING, VARNISHING, AND GILDING.

With plain Rules for the practice of every department of House and Sign Painting.

Colors, and How to Mix Them—Compound Colors—Oils—Varnishes—Polishes —Gilding Materials—Miscellaneous Materials—Grinding and Washing Colors—Cleanliness in Working—Practice of Painting—Practice of Varnishing and Polishing—Practice of Gilding—Instructions of Sign Writing —Harmony of Colors—Birds-Eye Maple in Distemper—Satin Wood—Mahogany in Distemper—Mahogany in Oil—Rose Wood.

This book is thorough in detail in every branch of Painting. By its aid every man can become his own Painter, in whatever kind of work he desires to undertake. **Price 25 Cents.**

THE AMATEUR PRINTER.

A work that should be in the hands of every one who desires to know anything about the art of Printing. It gives full instructions in all matters relating to the Setting of Type, enabling any one to become a proficient Printer. Fully Illustrated. **Price 25 Cents.**

THE ART OF VENTRILOQUISM.

Containing simple and full directions by which any one can acquire this amusing art. With numerous examples for practice. Also, instructions for making the **Magic Whistle**, for imitating birds, animals, and peculiar sounds of various kinds. Any boy who wishes to obtain an art by which he can develop a wonderful amount of astonishment, mystery and fun, should learn Ventriloquism, as he easily can, by following the simple secrets given in this book. The Magic Whistle is the same as is widely advertised and sold for Twenty-five Cents, while we will mail the book and method of making the Magic Whistle for only **15 Cents.**

NAPOLEON'S

ORACULUM AND COMPLETE BOOK OF FATE.

This is the celebrated Oracle of Human Destiny consulted by Napoleon the First previous to any of his undertakings, and by which he was so successful in war, business and love. It is the only authentic and complete copy extant, being translated into English from a German translation of an ancient Egyptian manuscript, found in 1801, by M. Sonnini, in one of the royal tombs near Mount Lybicus, in Upper Egypt. A curious work. Mailed for **15 Cts.**

THE COMPLETE

Fortune-Teller and Dream Book.

This book contains a Complete Dictionary of dreams alphabetically arranged, with a clear interpretation of each dream, and the Lucky Numbers that belong to it. It includes Palmistry, or Telling Fortunes by the Lines of the Hand; Fortune-Telling by the Grounds in a Tea or Coffee Cup; How to Read your Future Life by the White of an Egg; tells How to Know who your Future Husband will be, and how Soon You will be Married; Fortune-Telling by Cards; Hymen's Lottery; Good and Bad Omens. Mailed for **15 Cents.**

HOW TO TALK AND DEBATE.

A really valuable book, and one that every man and woman, boy and girl, should possess. Mailed for **15 Cents.**

"A MAN'S MANNERS MAKE HIS FORTUNE."

THE HANDBOOK

OF

GOOD MANNERS.

No work yet issued presents in so clear and intelligible a manner
the whole philosophy of etiquette. As its name implies,
it is a COMPLETE HANDBOOK on all matters
relating to behavior, and a guide in
everything appertaining to social intercourse of every
kind or form.

Among the matters treated of are—

DRESS,
INTRODUCTIONS,
CARDS,
SHAKING HANDS,
LETTERS AND PRESENTS,
CONVERSATION,
MORNING CALLS,
DINNER,
CARVING,
BALLS AND EVENING PARTIES,
LOVE, COURTSHIP, AND MARRIAGE,
RIDING AND DRIVING,
THE PROMENADE,
PUBLIC MEETINGS,
PICNICS,
BOATING,
STAYING WITH FRIENDS,
HINTS, &c., &c.

With this book, no one need be at a loss how to act in any
emergency that may arise, or hesitate to enter into any society
without being subject to confusion or discomfort.

Price, 20 Cents.

Sent to any address on receipt of price.

The only Book Published that really teaches the Art of Magic.

THE MAGICIAN'S GUIDE;
OR,
CONJURING MADE EASY.

Numerous books have been published professing to teach the Art of Magic, but without exception they have proved a delusion, being merely a compilation of disconnected experiments, often to the discouragement and disgust of the aspirant.

This work is written by a celebrated Magician, prompted with the honest desire to instruct those who wish to be initiated in the depths and mysteries of his art. In this he has been eminently successful. By a series of lessons, aided by illustrations, he has thoroughly explained and elucidated the principles of the science, and takes the learner through the whole field of

MAGIC, LEGERDEMAIN, and PRESTIDIGITATION,

INCLUDING TRICKS IN

Galvanism, Magnetism, and Electricity.

It gives also full and explicit directions for conducting an evening's entertainment, with a series of tricks and performances especially adapted for the amateur.

Any one who desires to be the sought and honored guest at every party, amusement, or entertainment, should not fail to possess this book, by which he can become in a short time as marvelous and mysterious as any of the great magicians and conjurors of the day.

Illustrated by Many First-Class Engravings.
PRICE—25 CENTS.

THE BLACK ART EXPOSED!

THE GREAT CHINESE WIZARD'S

HAND-BOOK OF MAGIC,
A BOOK OF WONDERS AND MYSTERIES UNVEILED.

It tells how to perform the most wonderful tricks, experiments and feats that have always and will ever continue to excite wonder, admiration, and awe in those who behold them. Among the wonders disclosed is the celebrated trick, never before published, viz: "How to Swallow an Unlimited Number of Needles and Thread," as performed by TUSANG, the great Chinese Magician. Also, the most celebrated tricks and arts as practiced by the most wonderful Magicians, Enchanters, and Conjurors of the day. This work exhibits the.

Wonders of Nature Magic	Wonders of Coin-handling	Wonders of Sleight of hand
Wonders of Chemistry	Wonders of White Magic	Wonders of Jugglery
Wonders of Electricity	Wonders of Galvanism	Wonders of Mechanics
Card Manipulation	Wonders of Magnetism	Wonders of Figures
	Wonders of Legerdemain.	

All adapted and explained for the amusement and delight of the home circle. It also contains THE ART OF MAKING FIREWORKS.

Printed on good paper, in a handsome illuminated cover.

PRICE—20 CENTS.
Sent by mail to any address on receipt of price.

THE BOOK OF KNOWLEDGE,

AND

Sure Guide to Rapid Wealth.

Fortunes are made every day by the manufacturing and selling of some of the articles here given. Directions are given for making all kinds of Cosmetics, Lotions, Ointments, Patent Medicines, Soaps, Cements, etc. The secrets used by Metal workers, how to make Gold, Silver and the various precious stones, with many practical directions for working and using the commoner metals. The secrets of the Liquor trade are fully detailed, and the choicest receipts and formulas are given for the making of different kinds of liquors, including the new method of making Cider without Apples, all without the use of poisons or poisonous drugs. It is arranged and divided into departments for the use of

Liquor Dealers,
Druggists,
Manufacturers,
Farmers,
Medical Men,

The Household,
Confectioners,
Hunters & Trappers,
Perfumers,
Artists.

No one, whatever be his position in life, can fail to find something in this book that will repay a hundredfold its price. Many of the receipts have been advertised and sold for sums ranging from 25 cents to ten dollars. We send the whole book, postage free, for 25 cents.

SINGING MADE EASY.

This book shows how any one with an ordinary voice can, by proper management, as here indicated, become proficient in singing. It explains the pure Italian method of producing and cultivating the voice, the management of the breath and voice organs, the best way of improving the ear, how to sing a ballad, with much other valuable information equally useful to Professional Singers and Amateurs. Price 20 cents.

RIDDLES, CONUNDRUMS AND PUZZLES.

The choicest, newest and best collection of Riddles, Conundrums, Charades, Enigmas, Anagrams, Rebusses, Transpositions, Puzzles, Problems, Paradoxes and other entertaining matter, ever published. Here is Fun for the Mirthful, Food for the Curious, and Matter for the Thoughtful. Price 20 cents.

A SURE GUIDE TO AUTHORSHIP!

KEY TO COMPOSITION;

OR,

HOW TO WRITE A BOOK.

As the title indicates, this book is

A COMPLETE GUIDE TO AUTHORSHIP,

AND

PRACTICAL INSTRUCTOR

IN ALL KINDS OF LITERARY LABOR.

Books heretofore published on these matters have taken it for granted that the learner has had some knowledge of the essentials of composition, and have given advice and instructions suitable only to those of some experience in Literary Composition. Other works have entirely neglected to give any

Information Relating to Publishing, Proof-Reading,

and other important matters relating to the getting up of books and placing them before the public. This book has carefully avoided these errors. It presumes, at the commencement, that the literary aspirant is totally ignorant of the construction of a composition, and commences at the first rudiments of the art, taking the learner from the construction of the most simple sentences gradually, but surely, to

The Most Elaborate Composition,

suitable for the highest kind of literary effort. The information given regarding Publishing, and the

COUNSELS TO YOUNG AUTHORS,

is valuable, and has never been given to the public before. As an Aid and Instructor to those who desire to follow literary pursuits permanently for profit, or to those who write for recreation and pleasure, the book is indispensable.

PRICE 30 CENTS.

Sent by mail, to any address, on receipt of price.

Hand-Book of Business,

AND

Complete Guide to all Kinds and Forms of Commercial and Mercantile Transactions, including a Dictionary of all the Terms and Technicalities used in Commerce and Business Houses.

There are also added many new and valuable methods of finding the cost of merchandise, and getting the correct solution of many matters constantly occurring in trade.

Correct legal forms are given of Bills, Deeds, Notes, Drafts, Cheques, Agreements, Receipts, Contracts, and other instruments of writing constantly necessary to every one, no matter in what calling he follows. Not only does it tell how to do Business, but it is a complete Book of Legal Knowledge. Its use will save many a dollar in lawyers' fees, and save much uncertainty and embarrassment to all who have occasion to give or receive any article of writing.

What the book tells:

It tells How to do Business—How to Conduct Mercantile Transactions by Sea or Land, at Home or in Foreign Countries—How to Keep a Bank Account—How to Make out Notes of all Kinds—How to Write an Agreement—How to Draw up Articles of Copartnership—How to Write a Bond—How to find out Profit and Loss on Goods—How to Make Out a Deed—How to Mark Goods (Private)—How to Write a Contract for Building—How to Write a Lease for Lands or Goods—How to Make Reports for all Kinds of Associations' Concerns and Business.

The book is indispensable to everybody, including—

Agents,	Clerks,	Lawyers.
Peddlers,	Book-Keepers,	Assessors.
Farmers,	Merchants,	Magistrates.
Mechanics,	Storekeepers,	Brokers.
Justices of the Peace.	Laborers,	Etc., etc.

All will find matter especially suited and needed by them. To the young man desirous of bettering his condition in life by engaging in merchandise, this book is worth its weight in gold. It is just what he needs. Its instructions will enable him to become proficient in the language of mercantile men, and also render him thoroughly competent to perform any duties that may devolve upon him in the Banking House, the Store, or the Office.

PRICE 25 CENTS.

Sent by mail, to any address, on receipt of price.

THE

HORSE-OWNER'S GUIDE,

AND

COMPLETE HORSE–DOCTOR.

This is a book that should be in the hands of every one who owns, works, or cares for a horse. It is a book that is needed— simple, concise, comprehensive, reliable, and practical—giving the fullest and best information on all matters that relate to this useful animal. Among its contents may be mentioned:

How to Select and Purchase a Horse.
Stable Management.
Condition.
General Arrangement of Stables.
Simple Rules for Shoeing.
Management of the Feet of Horses.
Causes of Disease, and its Prevention.
Breaking and Training of Horses.
Physiology of the Horse.
Breeding.
Care of Sucking Colts.
The Mare for a Farmer.
Diseases of Horses, Etc., Etc., Etc.

In preparing this work, the writer has provided for every possible exigency that may occur in the horse's career. The part devoted to the Diseases of the Horse is especially worthy of admiration, from its clearness, pointedness, and absence of unnecessary technicalities. More practical knowledge can be obtained of the anatomical structure, the cause and cure of disease, and the laws that govern and regulate health, by an hour's study, than months of reading through a dozen volumes, each costing three times the price of this.

The book is handsomely printed on good paper, illustrated with two very fine double-page engravings, representing the points of a horse and the diseases of the horse.

PRICE—FIFTY CENTS.

Sent by mail to any address on receipt of price.

"Dancing Made Easy."

BALL-ROOM DANCING
WITHOUT A MASTER,

AND

Complete Guide to the Ball-Room.

A book giving a simple description of the dances in popular use, free from the usual technicalities, has been long desired. To meet this want the publishers have engaged a celebrated professor and teacher of Dancing to write a book that shall supply this deficiency. In this the professor has been eminently successful. We may confidently assert that any one can, by the aid of this book, become proficient in the art of Ball-Room Dancing. The different dances are illustrated by diagrams and figures, making every step and variation quite clear and simple.

CONTENTS.

And many other popular dances.

Beautifully illustrated, and well printed. Price 25 cents Sent to any address on receipt of price.

THE ART OF
HUNTING, TRAPPING AND FISHING
MADE EASY,

BY AN OLD AND SUCCESSFUL HUNTER.

A Complete and Practical Guide for the use of the Amateur or Professional Hunter or Trapper.

This book will be found very valuable to those who have not had experience in these healthy, manly and profitable pursuits. The book is thorough in detail in every respect. The young sportsman can learn how to use the Gun or Rifle with ease and precision, and become an unerring shot. The mystery of making, setting and baiting Traps successfully, is shown.

The Best Methods of Catching all kinds of Fish,

Either in the Sea, Lake or River, is told practically and understandingly. The whole

Art of Managing and Training Dogs for Sporting Purposes,

and all about the care of Skins and Furs, so that they will fetch the highest market price, is given, with a vast amount of other valuable information relating to the Hunters Craft.

CONTENTS.

ABOUT GUNS.
HOW TO SELECT A GUN.
BREECH-LOADERS.
HOW TO LOAD A GUN.
THE ART OF GUNNING.
THE RIFLE, AND HOW TO USE IT.
ABOUT DOGS.
MANAGEMENT OF DOGS.
TRAINING OF DOGS.
BEST DOGS FOR SHOOTERS.
HUNTING, GUNNING AND SHOOTING.
RABBIT SHOOTING.
SNIPE SHOOTING.
PARTRIDGE SHOOTING,
WOODCOCK SHOOTING.
WILD FOWL SHOOTING.
DEER HUNTING.
BUFFALO HUNTING.

TRAPPING.
HOW TO MAKE TRAPS.
SETTING AND BAITING TRAPS.
PROPER SEASON FOR TRAPPING.
HINTS TO TRAPPERS.
SPECIFIC DIRECTIONS FOR TRAPPING AND SNARING ALL KINDS OF BIRDS AND ANIMALS.
FISHING.
BAITS, HOOKS, LINES, RODS, &c.
HOW TO CATCH VARIOUS KINDS OF FISH.
THE ART OF STRETCHING AND CURING SKINS.
DRESSING AND TANNING SKINS AND FURS.
COLORING AND DYEING SKINS AND FURS.

The Book is indispensable to all who delight to Fish, Hunt or Trap, either for sport or profit. The instructions will enable anyone to become thoroughly expert in the Sports and Pastimes of the River, Field or Forest. Illustrations are given, where needed, to elucidate matters, as in the construction of traps, &c.

This book will place many in a position to turn their spare time to a very profitable account. Furs and Skins are always in demand, and if properly caught and managed, sell for large prices.—**Price 25 Cents.**

TIT-BITS OF FUN,

FOR

JOLLY MORTALS.

Here are the portraits of two men who read two and a half pages of this Book of Phunniest of Phun. One expanded so much that his tailor bills have ruined him, and still his clothes are continually getting "tight." The other has been so exhilarated that there is danger of him never again becoming conscious of the realities of life.

We warrant this Book to be a sure cure for every ailment under and above the moon, sun, stars, and comets. It is a complete medley of Irish, Dutch, and Yankee Yarns, Blunders, and Bulls. It contains the richest gems of wit, the most laughable puns, outrageous drolleries, ludicrous burlesque, and side-splitting jokes, the newest stories, the most comical sells, and the raciest jests ; besides, there are lots of funny and irresistible pictures.

SPECIAL NOTICE.— Unless you want to laugh and get fat, don't send for it.

CAUTION.—Before buying, be sure to see that your buttons are O. K., and your ribs are not defective, because we assert, positively and emphatically, that we will not be responsible for damages.

Price, 25 Cents.

SONGS OF LOVE.

A very elegant collection of Love Songs and Heart Melodies. There are songs and poetic sentiments suitable for every phase of love's varied experience.—**Price 20 Cents.**

THE SPORT'S OWN SONGSTER.

A collection of the choicest, richest, spiciest, and raciest Songs and Ballads ever given to the fraternity. Suitable alike for humorous gatherings, jovial entertainments, "we won't go home till morning" meetings, and high old times generally. There are many new effusions never before published.—**Price 25 Cents.**

HONEST ABE'S JOKES.

This Book is a gem for those who can appreciate the keen repartee, the witty remark, or the pointed anecdote. It is a volume well worth preserving, as being a collection of the jokes, squibbs, and stories of President Lincoln.

Abraham Lincoln's character for jokes and "little stories" is too well known to need any explanatory remarks from us. It will be sufficient to know that these are his *bona fide* sayings, as fresh and racy as when they issued from his bosom, and are, as a whole, the most remarkable, pointed, and apt replies, illustrations and examples ever given to the world. They are perfect gems of wit and humor. They sparkle like brilliants of the first water, and not one single example in the whole collection is ever dull, pointless, or even doubtful. They are all pungent, unequivocal, and original, related in that peculiar, characteristic, and irresistible style that only Abraham Lincoln could use. Illustrated with portrait of Honest Abe, and also with four scenes in his career, representing him as a backwoodsman, as a volunteer in the Black Hawk war, as a raftsman, and as a rail-splitter.—**Price 50 Cents.**

BOOK-KEEPING MADE EASY.

Few will question the importance of a correct knowledge of keeping accounts, but there is, probably, no branch of education so generally neglected or on which so much ignorance is manifested. The total neglect of it in our Public Schools and the lengthy, wordy, and cumbersome treatises that have been written with the object of teaching it, may cause this state of things.

Book-keeping is a very simple art, and can readily be mastered by any one of ordinary capacity in a very short time. In any business, however small, a knowledge of book-keeping is indispensable. This book is just the one needed by the learner, being simple, thorough, and practical. Its teachings will enable any one to acquire the whole art of book-keeping, both by single and double entry.—**Price 25 Cents.**